Two Pennies

Australian children rebuild a French school after World War I

Vicki Bennett
Illustrated by John Flitcroft

First published 2015

Cataloguing-in-Publication entry available at the National Library of Australia

Creator: Bennett, Vicki, author.
Title: Two pennies / Vicki Bennett ; illustrated by John Flitcroft.
ISBN: 9781925046816 (paperback)
Target Audience: For primary school age.
Subjects: McGregor, Henry George.
Boys--Australia--Conduct of life.
Schools--France--Villers-Bretonneux--Juvenile literature.
Reconstruction (1914-1939)--France--Villers-Bretonneux--Juvenile literature.
Australia--Relations--France--Villers-Bretonneux--Juvenile literature.
Villers-Bretonneux (France)--Relations--Australia--Juvenile literature.
Other Creators/Contributors: Flitcroft, John, illustrator.
Dewey Number: 920.710994

Published by Boolarong Press, Salisbury, Brisbane, Australia.
www.boolarongpress.com.au

Printed and bound by Watson Ferguson & Company, Salisbury, Australia

*For George's great-grandchildren
Adelaide, Arlo, Finlay, Grace, Liam,
Oliver and Riley.*

When George was a little boy he had a scooter, a small wooden truck and a set of dominos his grandfather had given him. He lived with his Mum, his brother and his two sisters above their bakery.

Early in the mornings, George would smell the warm, rich aroma of the bread as it came hot and steaming from the big ovens in the bakery.

One day, George's mother asked him to put on his good clothes. After his brother and sisters had left for school, they caught the tram to the docks.

He couldn't remember ever seeing his mother so happy and skipped cheerfully along beside her.

A big ship had just arrived and was unloading trucks and cars and thousands of soldiers, back from the First World War. The soldiers were streaming towards them.

Suddenly through the crowd, head and shoulders above the others, appeared a tall soldier with jet-black hair. George recognised Henry, his Dad, from the photo on the mantelpiece. There he was walking towards them, home from the War in France.

They ran to meet him and Henry lifted George high above his head and sat him on his shoulders. There George stayed all the way home.

When George was a little older he noticed that his Dad was often sad. It was as if a big dark cloud was following him around. Sometimes he would find his Dad alone in his study, staring into space.

So he asked his father, "What's wrong Daddy? Why are you so sad?"

Henry told him that when he was fighting in the War, bombs destroyed many villages in France and he was sad because little girls and boys George's age had no schools to go to.

George thought and thought about the girls and boys in France.

One morning, the Headmaster on school parade announced they were going to raise money to build a school in a little village called Villers-Bretonneux (Vill-ers Bret-ton-ner) in France. Many battles involving Australian soldiers had taken place there.

George was so excited. If every child in the school raised two pennies, it would help to build the school in France!

Later, when George and his brother and sisters sat eating their dinner, he announced his plan. "I am going to find a job so that I can raise two pennies to build a school in France."

His brother and sisters teased him, "But George, you are only five years old, you can't get a job."

"Oh yes I can!" said George sitting up very tall and puffing out his chest. "You just watch me!"

His brother and sisters laughed. But afterwards when all the dishes were washed and dried and put away, his mother asked him to go into his father's study.

He opened the door. The lights were blazing and his Dad's face was beaming.

His Dad said, "If you can wake up very early every morning to feed the horses and get them ready to deliver the bread, you can earn enough money to help build the school."

George smiled a big, wide, happy smile and said, "You can count on me, Dad."

Every day George rose early to care for the horses. First, he led them from the stables, put their bridles over their necks and tethered them to the horse rail outside.

Then he fed each of them a bucket of oats, so they would have full stomachs to do their day's work.

After the horses had delivered the bread, George washed and brushed their coats so they were clean and shiny.

Soon he had earned his first two pennies.

The children were very excited to bring their pennies to school. The Headmaster calculated that if they placed all the pennies end-to-end, it would make a line that would stretch a mile long.

So each child proudly placed their two pennies end-to-end, stretching around the school like a shiny snake.

The school at Villers-Bretonneux in France was named The Victoria School, after all the children in Victoria, Australia who helped to build it.

SCHOOL

George kept working early mornings with the horses and very soon he had earned another two pennies. He put these away in his secret box under the bed.

He dreamt of visiting the Victoria school in France. But after the War, life was hard. Men and women couldn't get work so it was difficult to feed their families.

George's father was a kind man. When some of his customers didn't have money for food, he gave them bread, cake and buns so they could eat.

George's father needed him to help in the bakery. There was no money to spend on a long trip to France.

George grew up and left home. He married his sweetheart Vida, and they had two children of their own.

They were very happy, but times were still tough. There was still no money for a trip to France.

Finally, in 1982 George wrote a letter to the Mayor in Villers-Bretonneux, to ask if he and his wife could visit.

"Yes," was the Mayor's reply, "it would be a great honour to have you visit the school."

It took 23 hours to fly to Paris, then two more hours on the train to the village.

George and Vida had never been on such an adventure.

It was a bright, sunny day with an aqua blue sky when the big, black train pulled in to the platform at Villers-Bretonneux.

George was thrilled to finally be there, and on what seemed to be a festival day. A brass band was playing music and children were dressed in their Sunday best.

George and Vida gathered their luggage and stepped onto the busy platform.

A man in a fine red coat with brass buttons and medals around his neck approached them and spoke excitedly in French. "Madame, Monsieur, suivez-moi, s'il vous plait."

They did not understand what the man was saying, so they smiled and kept walking.

S BRETONNEUX

DO NOT FORGET AUSTRALIA

Suddenly out of the crowd stepped an Englishman who said, "The Mayor is welcoming you to the village and would like you to go with him to the school. They are very happy to see you."

"Is this band for us?" asked George.

"Oui Monsieur," said the Mayor proudly, as he guided George and Vida to the Victoria School. The band followed, playing loudly.

The schoolchildren were on parade singing Waltzing Matilda when they arrived.

George was bursting with happiness to finally see the school that he had helped to build.

Many years later when George was an old man, his daughter came to visit him. He opened a small wooden box, took two pennies and placed them into her hand.

George said to his daughter, "Of all the pennies I raised when I was a little boy, I have kept these two. I want you to take them to the village in France and give them to the school for me."

George's daughter flew in a big aeroplane to France and found the little school in the village that her father had helped to build.

These two pennies are now proudly displayed in the French-Australian Museum in Villers-Bretonneux. They tell the story of a little boy who had a dream and made it come true.

This photo of Vicki and her father George was taken in 2010.

Vicki Bennett is an artist and an author of twenty-three books, translated into numerous languages around the world. www.vickibennett.com.au

Henry George McGregor, known as George, served his country in Borneo and Papua New Guinea during the Second World War. Returning to Australia, he ran several businesses and was a Councillor for the Geelong City Council.

He moved to Brisbane with his family in 1956, where he settled and became a District Inspector for the State Government Insurance Office until his retirement.

George served as a Return Services League State Councillor for over 30 years. As a Foundation Member and Chairman of the Community Services Committee, he helped buy the land for RSL Fairview Residential Care, Pinjarra Hills, where he lived happily for two years until his death in 2012. He was a driving force behind the "Girl in a Million" contest and at the local RSL level he held various offices at the Clayfield-Toombul Sub-branch. He was also Foundation President of the Queensland Diabetes Association and was awarded the OAM in 1989.

With his natural ear for music, he played the piano every day. When he was little, he listened to his sister practise and would play the pieces precisely by ear, including any mistakes she had made. He whistled perfectly in tune.

George lived much as he does in this book, showing courage and persistence throughout his life. He remained resilient and hearty to the end. He shared his sense of humour willingly and always exhibited joy and dignity to those around him. He never tired of telling the story of his two pennies. This book is his story.

The illustrator, John Flitcroft, has a science background, but his passion is drawing. This is his first book and his beautiful illustrations bring George's story to life. www.johnflitcroft.com